PLEASE READ TO ME.
A Round-the-Year Storybook

Elizabeth Rodger

Copyright © 2002 by Elizabeth Rodger.

Published by Troll Communications L.L.C.

Printed in the United States of America.   ISBN 0-8167-7593-1

10 9 8 7 6 5 4 3 2 1

JANUARY: Dan's Resolution

Dan Dog watched as Mother Dog hung a new calendar on the kitchen wall.

"Why do we need a new calendar?" asked Dan.

"This is the first day of January, the beginning of a new year," explained Mother Dog.

"What's so special about January first?" asked Dan.

"It's the best day to make a resolution," said Mother.

"What's a resolution?" asked Dan.

"A resolution is a decision to try to do better, like keeping your room tidy," said Mother Dog.

Dan knew there were many things he could do better. Choosing one thing to improve upon would be tough! He decided to think about a resolution tomorrow. Today, he wanted to have fun sledding with his best friend, Mattie.

The doorbell rang. "Hello! Dan, are you there?" called Mattie.

Dan pulled on his snowsuit and boots, and he grabbed his sled. He noticed a big brown paper bag sitting on Mattie's sled.

"What's in the bag?" Dan asked.

"Some vegetable soup, and my mother's best fruit bread," said Mattie. "I'm taking them to the Possums. They're sick with bad colds."

Father Possum opened the door when Mattie rang the bell. He was wrapped in a heavy robe. His nose and eyes were red, and he couldn't stop sniffling. He thanked Mattie, and he said the soup was sure to make his family feel much better.

As the good friends went on their way, Dan noticed Mattie was smiling a special smile.

The big hill was busy when the two friends arrived. Sleds and toboggans whizzed down the slope. Dan and Mattie joined the happy crowd.

As they reached the bottom of the slope after their first run, they noticed Father Bear trying to comfort his little daughter, Bippy.

"I want!" she wailed, reaching toward the hill. Father Bear explained to Bippy that he would get her a sled when she was older. But Bippy wanted to ride on one now.

"Would you like to borrow mine?" asked Mattie. "I can share with Dan."

Bippy's crying turned to giggles as Father Bear sat on the sled with her for a few runs down the slope. Mattie watched them, smiling that special smile again.

Soon it was time to go home. As the friends passed Grandma Badger's house, Mattie noticed her mailbox was full. Her walkway had not been cleared of snow.

"I wonder if Grandma is okay," said Mattie, emptying the mailbox. He knocked on her door. Grandma appeared and gratefully accepted the mail.

"Thank you, my young friend," she said. "I was afraid I'd fall in the snow."

"If you have shovels, we'll clear your walkway," offered Mattie.

Grandma handed shovels to the friends, and they got to work. As they cleared the snow, Dan smiled a special smile. Being kind made him feel so good.

When Dan returned home, he announced he had decided his resolution for the New Year.

"I will be as kind as Mattie," said Dan.

"That's a wonderful resolution. I'm proud of you," said Mother Dog, giving Dan a big hug.

FEBRUARY: The Biggest Heart

Valentine's Day was coming.

Charlie announced that he wanted to send a valentine card to someone special. He asked Mother if she could buy one for him.

"Why don't you make one instead?" said Mother Pig. "I have pretty red and pink paper, scissors, glue, and crayons you can use."

Charlie thought for a moment.

"Okay," he agreed. "My card will be the best Valentine's Day card ever."

Charlie gathered the supplies, went into his room, and sat at his desk. He was ready to make a card for a special person. But Charlie couldn't decide who was special. He needed Mother's advice. She was busy sewing.

"I want to send a card to a special person. What kind of person is special?" he asked.

"Send your card to someone with a big heart," said Mother.

"How will I know if the person has a big heart?" asked Charlie.

"Kind people have big hearts," said Mother.

Charlie thought this over. He was sure Miss Possum, his teacher, had a big heart. Bertie Bear was kind. Missy was kind, too. She always shared her cookies at lunch. Although she was small, Charlie was sure she had a big heart. Officer Barney always had a big smile for the children at the crosswalk. He took such care to keep them safe. He was certainly kind enough to have a big heart.

Charlie could think of so many people with big hearts. Who was the most special? He needed Father's advice.

"Send the card to the kindest person you know," said Father.

Charlie went back to his desk and thought some more. After some time, Mother and Father

At bedtime, Charlie was tired from his efforts. He snuggled happily into his bed. Father hugged Charlie and wondered why he was smiling.

In the morning, Mother got up early. She stepped on a big red heart outside her bedroom door. Charlie must have dropped it, she thought.

She was very wrong! Oh my! She could hardly believe what she saw. Charlie *had* been busy. There were cards everywhere. One taped to the oven said, "Thank you for the yummy pies and cookies." Another on the refrigerator said, "Thank you for hugging away the hurts." A card stuck to the washing machine said, "Thank you for washing all my muddy clothes." Mother Pig giggled when she found a little heart attached to her toothbrush.

Charlie had a big smile on his face when he came to breakfast. "Happy Valentine's Day," he said, giving Mother his biggest and prettiest card. It said, "For the best Mom, with the biggest heart of all. Love, Charlie."

wondered why Charlie was so quiet. They peeked into his room. Cards were scattered over the floor.

"Oh my! He must be sending a card to every kind person in town," whispered Mother.

MARCH: A Breezy Day

The Squirrel twins, Pippy and Tammy, peered out the window. Tree branches swayed. Leaves fluttered in the wind. The breezy days of March had arrived.

"Let's play in the wind," said Tammy.

"No, thanks. The wind ruffles my fur and makes my nose itch," said Pippy.

"If I promise you fun and a big surprise, will you come out to play?" asked Tammy.

"Oh, all right," agreed Pippy. "I hope the wind doesn't ruffle my fur and tickle my nose."

Tammy held up a flat package. "This is the surprise!" she said. "It's a secret until we get to a special place."

The twins set off. Pippy plodded along with her head hanging so low that she tripped a few times.

"Careful! I don't want the surprise to break," said Tammy.

"And I don't want my nose to be tickled," muttered Pippy, continuing to walk with her head hanging low.

They heard laughter and happy voices as they neared the big meadow.

"Pippy, look up!" exclaimed Tammy.

Pippy lifted her head enough to peek in the direction of Tammy's pointing paw. She forgot about the wind tickling her nose as she raised her head to admire the many beautiful kites fluttering in the breeze. Lots of the twins' friends were having fun in the March winds.

"I know what's in the package," Pippy said excitedly.

The twins unwrapped a pretty acorn kite, laid it on the ground, and unwound some string.

"Let's run and launch it," said Tammy.

The acorn kite fluttered off the ground and climbed as the wind lifted it higher and higher, its long tail swishing from side to side.

Pippy shouted, "Hold on, Tammy! This is fun," not caring how much the wind was blowing in her face.

They let out more string. Just then, a strong gust blew. The kite surged upward, higher and higher, to join the other kites.

"Oh! The wind is tickling my nose. I have to scratch it," cried Tammy, letting go of the string.

"You can't let go. I can't hold the kite all by myself," shouted Pippy. The kite dragged her across the ground and lifted her into the air.

She held the string tightly as she screamed, "Help me! I'm being carried away."

"Hang on! We'll save you," yelled Bertie Bear as he and other good friends gave chase.

The little squirrel held on as she swooped high and low. Bertie leaped and almost caught her foot as the chase zigzagged across the meadow.

But Pippy's cry for help quickly changed to a giggle of delight. She was flying!

"Wheeee! Look at me," she called.

As suddenly as it started, the gust of wind died down. Pippy landed softly on the ground, still holding the string.

"Are you hurt, Pippy?" Bertie asked.

"I feel wonderful! Did you see? I was flying," exclaimed Pippy.

Everyone laughed, quite relieved that no harm had come to the little squirrel.

From that day, Pippy realized that March winds, even if they ruffled fur and tickled noses, could be lots of fun.

APRIL: An Easter Secret

Father Pig was preparing an Easter egg hunt for his children, Sally, Toby, and Charlie.

After breakfast, the Pig children got their baskets and rushed outside. Charlie noticed an egg lying on the doorstep.

"This is a special egg. It comes apart," said Mother. "Look, there's a message inside. It says, 'Take ten steps forward. Then look up!'"

"One, two, three," counted the Pig children as they moved forward.

"There's a special egg in the tree house. I'll get it," said Toby.

The clue inside the egg said, "Find a tall tree. Turn it around."

"The old spruce is the tallest tree," said Sally.

"We can't turn the tree around. But we can go around to the other side," said Toby, rushing ahead.

What a sight! Lots of chocolate eggs, wrapped in bright glittering paper, nestled on the lowest branches of the old spruce. Brightly painted eggs lay in the grass.

The children popped the eggs into their baskets.

Sally found another special egg. The clue said, "Cheep! Cheep! Cheep! We live in the box where your letters go."

"Postie puts letters in our mailbox," said Sally. The pig children rushed to the mailbox.

Wow! It was filled with yellow marshmallow chickens. A special egg was stuffed in the back of the mailbox.

"Hurry, Mom, read the clue," said Charlie.

"'Find a surprise behind something that is very big and very hard,'" said Mother, reading the clue.

"The rock by the maple tree is very big and very hard," Charlie said. He set off at a run, followed by Sally and Toby. As the children reached the rock, a floppy-eared figure jumped out with a loud "Boo!" It was the Easter Bunny!

"Hello, children. I have one more treat for you," said the Easter Bunny, reaching into a basket to give a big chocolate bunny to each Pig child.

"I've never had such a big chocolate bunny," said Charlie as he wrapped his arms around the knees of the Easter Bunny to give him a hug.

"What a nice little pig," said the Easter Bunny.

The children watched the Easter Bunny hop away, huffing and puffing, his ears bobbing wildly. He turned his head and shouted over his shoulder, "Have a happy Easter"—and stumbled and flopped onto his round tummy! He struggled to his feet and immediately flopped onto his back. He gave a squeaky little giggle as he flapped his arms and wiggled his long ears. Then he hopped, bobbed, and stumbled out of sight. The children agreed that the Easter Bunny was the clumsiest, silliest bunny they had ever seen.

Mother Pig and the children made their way home. Charlie noticed a furry something lying on the doorstep.

"It's the Easter Bunny's tail," said Toby. "How did it get here?"

"I think Daddy was the Easter Bunny," said Sally. "The tail fell off his costume."

The children giggled, remembering how very clumsy their father had been as the Easter Bunny. They decided not to tell Father Pig he had been discovered. It would be their Easter secret.

MAY: A Higgledy-Piggledy Patch

Pansy enjoyed watching her father work in his garden. He planted vegetable seeds in neat, straight rows. He stapled each empty seed packet to a piece of wood stuck in the ground to remind him what grew there.

Pansy was delighted when he invited her to help.

"You can plant the flower patch. And I've got just the tools you'll need," said Father Possum, presenting her with a spade, a rake, and a wheelbarrow that were the perfect size for a small gardener.

Pansy used her spade to turn the soil. She raked the soil flat. The patch was ready for planting. She tore the top off each seed packet and arranged the packets on the ground in neat rows.

She stood back to admire her work. Just then, a gust of wind blew through the garden. It picked up the packets and tossed them around, spilling the seeds all over the patch.

"Oh, no!" cried Pansy. "Look, Daddy. The wind scattered the seeds all over my patch. The flowers won't grow in neat rows. My garden won't look nice."

"Don't cry, Pansy. A higgledy-piggledy flower patch can look very pretty," said Father Possum. "In the meantime, you can guess what types of flowers you'll have when the seeds sprout. Let's rake the soil to cover the seeds."

Pansy smiled. She carefully saved the packets to remind her of what flowers might grow.

In time, little green plants sprouted in the patch. Pansy watered her garden every few days. Some plants grew fast, and the leaves took different shapes. Pansy looked at the pictures of the flowers and their leaves on the seed packets. Then she matched the shapes of the leaves to what she saw in her garden.

"Look, Daddy! I think these plants are daisies. These are zinnias. Those are sunflowers," she said.

"Well done, Pansy," said Father Possum.

Leaves climbed up the trellis at the entrance to the flower patch. One day, a blue flower blossomed among the leaves. Another blossomed. Soon there was an archway of beautiful morning glories. The patch was becoming a blaze of color. Petunias and marigolds formed brilliant clumps. Foxgloves, black-eyed Susans, and daisies swayed in the gentle breeze, a sea of pink, yellow, red, and white. Sunflowers gathered around the garden bench, creating a tall canopy of shade.

Father Possum spent lots of time in the flower patch. He liked to sit in the shade of the giant sunflowers, reading a favorite book.

"I think you like my flower patch, Daddy," said Pansy.

"I think your flower patch is the most beautiful higgledy-piggledy patch ever," Father Possum replied.

JUNE: The Topsy-Turvy Birthday

"Oh, what a sleepyhead!"

Justin's eyes snapped open at the sound of his mother's voice. He sat up in bed, wide awake and excited. This was his special day, his birthday.

After breakfast, the Beaver family prepared for Justin's party. Streamers, pennants, and balloons were draped from trees. A hammock, filled with balloons, was hung high between two trees. Party hats, favors, and presents were arranged on a long table.

Soon the Raccoons and Wally Woodchuck arrived, and it was party time! Everyone had fun playing London Bridge, Blind Man's Bluff, and musical chairs.

"Listen, everyone," shouted Father Beaver. "Whoever bursts the most balloons chooses the next game." He pulled a string attached to the hammock. Balloons spilled out and floated slowly to the ground, where eager little hands pounced on them. *Pop! Pop!* went the

sounds of bursting balloons amid screams of
laughter.

Justin's brother, Kenny, popped the most
balloons. "Let's play Follow the Leader," he said.
"Here we go! Follow me around the tree. Put
your arms up high. Put your arms down low. Hop
on your right foot. Then hop on your left."

Justin had trouble hopping from one foot to
the other. So he hopped on both feet and flopped
onto his back in mud. He picked himself up.

"What's the matter, my little friend?" Wally
asked. Justin turned for Wally to see his dirty back.
"Cheer up, Justin. The sun will dry the mud."

When everyone had eaten birthday cake,
Wally played a snappy tune on his harmonica.

Kenny asked to play the harmonica.

"I want to play it," said Nellie.

"What about me! Me!" shouted the other children.

"We'll have a race to decide who gets to play,"
said Wally. "Run to the big tree, and then come
back to me. Ready! On your mark, get set, go!"
The children raced toward the tree. Nellie was
first to get back to Wally (raccoons run so much
faster than beavers). Justin, being the smallest
beaver, came in last.

Wally felt sorry for Justin. "I declare this to be

a topsy-turvy race," he said. "Justin came in last. He is the birthday boy, and he gets to play the harmonica." Everyone agreed, and Nellie cheered loudest for Justin.

But before Justin could start to play, the sun moved behind a dark cloud and it began to rain.

"Run for cover," shouted Father Beaver. Wally didn't see the muddy patch as he ran. Swoosh! He slipped and landed on his stomach.

The rain soon stopped and the sun shone again.

"Look at us," said Wally. "Justin has a dirty back, and I have a dirty front. What a topsy-turvy pair

we are!" Everyone laughed. "Now, my little topsy-turvy friend, it's time to make music."

Justin put the harmonica to his mouth. Puffing into the instrument, he played a lively tune.

"Wow! That sounds good. You are a terrific musician, Justin," said Wally. He clapped a beat, and everyone danced to Justin's music.

The next day, Mother Beaver found a package on the doorstep. The card read, "For Justin, a wonderful musician. Your topsy-turvy friend."

Justin opened the package and found a little harmonica inside. You can guess who sent it.

JULY: Proud to Be Me!

William Robert was a little pig. Everyone called him Billybob. He was usually a happy little pig, but today Billybob was not happy. He was afraid to march in the town parade the next day because he thought he was too clumsy. Sometimes he got in Mother's way. Sometimes big brother Sammy told Billybob he was too little to do things. And sometimes Billybob made a mess, even when he was trying hard to be neat.

Billybob decided to go fly his kite instead of worrying about the parade. He found a nice flat patch of grass. He started to run. The kite fluttered higher and higher. Flump! Billybob fell onto his round tummy. Swish! Swoosh! The kite fluttered lower and lower. Flump! It landed on Billybob's head.

I'm such a clumsy little pig, he thought. I'm just a bother to everyone. Poor Billybob began to cry.

"Don't cry, Billybob. Your kite can be fixed," said a kind voice. It was Officer Barney. "You should be happy thinking about marching in the parade tomorrow."

Who would want a clumsy little pig in the parade? Billybob was not happy at the thought.

The next morning, Billybob was awakened by a noise outside. Father Pig was pulling a golden coach from his workshop. Mother and Father Pig, Sammy, and sister Daisy were wearing costumes.

"Do I get to wear a costume?" called Billybob.

"Of course! You're going to wear a band uniform like Daddy's," replied Mother. "You've been chosen to lead the parade."

Billybob worried about being leader. He was such a clumsy little pig. Everyone would laugh at him.

What a sight when the Pigs arrived in town! Billybob had never seen so many people. Everyone was excited and happy as they greeted old friends, admired costumes, and chattered loudly, waiting for the parade to begin.

Then Father Pig blew his whistle for everyone to get into position. Billybob moved closer to him and grabbed his coattail. With a "left, right, left," Father Pig led the parade toward Main Street as Billybob shuffled behind him, holding tightly to his coattail.

A big crowd lined the route of the parade and clapped with delight at the wonderful marching band. Oompa! Oompa! Tootle-toot! Pip! Pip! Boom-biddy-boom! Sammy was doing wonderful cartwheels. Clowns did somersaults, chased each other with brooms, and gave balloons to the

laughing, cheering crowd. Princess Daisy came last in the parade, sitting in the golden coach with a golden crown on her head. Flower girls scattered rose petals as dancers skipped and twirled before her carriage.

Above the laughter and cheering, Billybob heard, "Look at that little pig! Isn't he adorable! What a handsome little fellow."

Oh! Could it be? They're talking about me, thought Billybob. They think I'm handsome.

Billybob let go of Father's coattail and stepped out to lead the parade. With his head high and his arms swinging, he marched smartly down Main Street. The crowd clapped and cheered, delighted with the efforts of the little pig.

Spectators joined the parade behind Princess Daisy's carriage, and everyone marched to the great meadow for a wonderful picnic.

Billybob spotted a big bear boy making his way through the crowd toward him.

"You looked so smart," said the big bear boy.

"Thank you! I'm proud to be me," said Billybob, happy because he didn't feel like a clumsy little pig anymore.

AUGUST: So Very Hot!

It was a hot August day. Postie Possum plodded along Bramble
Way, stopping to stuff envelopes and packages into mailboxes.
Dust covered his feet as he tramped slowly and wearily along.
It was so very hot.

He found Mother Bear and her children in a hammock under
two big shade trees. A fly buzzed lazily above them. The hammock
was quite still. Not one of the Bears moved to chase the fly away.
Not one of the Bears came to collect the mail. It was so very hot.

Farther along, Milton Mouse was trying to stay cool. He sat on
his porch, pulling a string that wafted a big leaf back and forth.
On seeing Postie, he got up slowly and went to collect his mail.

"Would you like a glass of lemonade?" Milton asked. Postie
gratefully accepted his friend's offer. When he had sipped the
cool drink, he thanked Milton for his kindness and, feeling
greatly refreshed, went on his way.

As Postie approached the Beaver home, he heard laughter and
sounds of play echoing from the trees. He had to see who could be
so silly as to play in this heat. He plodded through the woods to
where a dam had been built across the stream. Beyond the dam,
a beautiful pond glittered in the sunlight. Mother and Father

Beaver were sitting at the edge with their feet dangling in the cool water. Their children were having fun pushing a ball around the pond.

"You look so hot, Postie," said Mother Beaver. "Come and dip your feet in the pond."

As he sat with his feet dangling in the water, Postie had an idea. "I think all our friends need to cool off in this heat. Would you share your pond for a day?" he asked.

"That's a wonderful idea," said Father Beaver. "We could invite everyone over tomorrow for a picnic."

"I'll spread the word," said Postie.

The next day, Postie arrived early to help with the preparations. But the Beavers had things under control. They had cut down branches to build tables and benches. Pennants and streamers hung from the trees. A shallow area of the pond had been roped off to make a place where the infants could play. It all looked colorful and festive.

Postie sat in the shade, waiting for the guests to arrive. Soon some friends came along, walking slowly through the woods, carrying picnic hampers and whining infants. Older children, hot and grumpy, straggled behind. It was so very hot.

The grumbling stopped when they emerged from the trees. The youngsters' eyes sparkled at the sight of Beaver Pond. Sun hats and shirts were ripped off as children rushed to be the first one in the water.

Officer Barney was desperate to take a dip. He couldn't drag his eyes from the glistening water. "Why don't you swim with the children while I set out the picnic?" Mother Bear offered with a knowing smile.

Officer Barney quickly pulled off his shirt and shouted to the Bear children, "Beat you into the pond!" He did a giant belly flop into the middle of the pool. What a splash! There was laughter all around as water sprayed over everyone. It felt so wonderfully cool.

Officer Barney was right in the middle of the fun. Children gathered around him, pleading to be thrown high in the air so they could land with a big splash. Only Pig's nose and round tummy showed as he floated. Infants paddled and splashed at the edge of the pond. Milton Mouse took to the water sitting in a little tube. It was a happy sight.

As evening fell, the residents gathered their belongings. Postie watched as they left, slowly winding their way through the trees to Bramble Way. They looked so very cool on this hot August evening. Postie smiled as he listened to the laughter echoing through the woods.

The picnic had been a great success.

SEPTEMBER: Where's Milton?

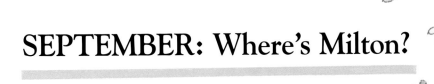

Milton Mouse lived in a hollow at the foot of a tall maple tree. He liked to sit on his porch and wave friendly greetings to his neighbors. Mooley Mole stopped often for an evening chat. Chippy Chipmunk, Wharton Toad, and Bucky Squirrel were also regular visitors.

Autumn arrived. Leaves turned yellow and red and began to fall. It was time to gather seeds and nuts for the long winter. One day, as Milton moved through the woods filling his basket, drops of rain fell. Milton picked up a leaf and scuttled home, holding his makeshift umbrella to stay dry.

The wind began to howl as the storm grew. Milton ate supper. Then he went to bed, hoping to get an early start in the morning to harvest more seeds and nuts.

Hours later, he woke. Finding his house still dark, he went back to sleep. He awoke again several hours later, and all was still dark. Once more, he went back to sleep.

The afternoon sun was shining brightly. Mooley Mole was wandering down the trail to check on his good friend. He came to the spot where Milton's house should have been. There was nothing there but a thick carpet of leaves. He wandered up and down, but Milton's house was nowhere to be seen. He ran to find Wharton Toad and Chippy Chipmunk.

"Milton's house is missing! I can't find him," he said to Wharton and Chippy. They returned with Mooley along the trail.

"Milton is missing. Have you seen him?" they asked Bucky Squirrel and Freddie Raccoon.

"No, we haven't seen him, but we'll join the search," said Bucky and Freddie.

They all called loudly for Milton.

There was no reply.

Meanwhile, Milton sat up in bed and was very surprised to see it was *still* dark. It seemed such a long night, and he was so hungry. A big plate of pancakes would be yummy. He fired up his little stove and added some logs.

Outside, the friends were losing hope of finding Milton.

"I smell smoke! Look," said Mooley, pointing to where smoke rose from the leaves at the base of the tall maple. Freddie pushed the leaves aside, exposing a chimney. Then he cleared more leaves.

Milton was about to take a bite of pancake when a shaft of sunshine streaked into his house. He fell off his stool as Freddie peered through his window.

Milton ran to his door, puzzled.

"What is going on?" he asked his friends as he opened the door.

"You were missing, Milton," said Mooley. "The leaves covered up your house."

Everyone had a good laugh.

"Thank you for finding me," said Milton. "I made pancakes. Would you like to join me?"

The friends happily accepted.

OCTOBER: Who Doesn't Like Treats?

Halloween had arrived. The Possum children could hardly wait to go from house to house, filling their bags with goodies.

"What if we meet monsters?" asked Patty.

"I'll take my bell and ring it loudly," said big sister Pansy.

"My trumpet should scare them. Monsters will run at the first toot," said big brother Peter.

Patty peered outside. O-o-oh! The tall trees cast dark shadows in the moonlight. It looked so scary! Patty didn't move.

"Are monsters behind the trees?" she asked.

"Not for long," said Pansy, ringing her bell. *Tootle-toot-toot* went Peter on his trumpet.

As Father and the children set off, a scary sound came from above. *Too-whit-too-whoo.*

"Ooooo-o-oh!" exclaimed Patty, grabbing Father and holding on tightly.

Pansy rang her bell. *Tootle-toot* went Peter on his trumpet.

"It's just a wise old owl," said Father.

Suddenly, horrible creatures appeared from the dark, shadowy trees.

"Eeeeek!" yelled Pansy as she rang her bell loudly. Peter blew hard on his trumpet, and Patty hid behind Father and clutched his coat. The horrible creatures didn't run away. A ghost nodded and smiled at Pansy ringing her bell.

What a surprise when the horrible creatures took off their masks! It was fun to see the faces of good friends. The friendly ghost was the only one who didn't show its face. How very strange!

Father and the children went on their way. But someone was following them. It was the friendly ghost who didn't show its face.

Pansy rang her bell. Peter blew on his trumpet. The ghost just smiled, and waved, and nodded its head. It didn't run away.

"It's so very friendly. It can't be a real ghost," said Pansy.

The ghost followed them to Betsy Bear's house. Betsy gave the children candied apples. What a shock when the ghost didn't take one.

"Wow! And Betsy's are the best," said Peter.

The ghost didn't take any taffy from Billy Badger. Murphy Mouse had fudge. She offered some to the ghost, but it didn't take any. Wherever they went, the ghost never took any treats. How very strange!

"Wow!" said Peter. "Who doesn't like treats?"

"I know who the ghost is," said Patty. "It's Mommy. She looks so silly."

"How do you know that?" asked Pansy.

"She never eats sweet treats," said Patty.

"We'll pretend we don't know who she is while she follows us." Pansy giggled as the ghost waved, and smiled, and nodded its head.

Father and the children returned home with bags filled with goodies. But something was wrong. Mother was waiting to greet them. The children turned to see the ghost wave, then disappear into the darkness.

Oh my! Was it possible? Do you think it could have been . . . a real ghost?

You can be sure someone knew.

Too-whit-too-whoo!

NOVEMBER: Let Us Give Thanks!

Mother Dog was busy planning Thanksgiving dinner. She made a list of the ingredients she needed to cook her family's favorite foods. Father Dog loved pumpkin pie, so she wrote "Pumpkin" at the top of her list.

At The Pumpkin Patch, Mother saw a notice that said, "CLOSED FOR WINTER." There were no pumpkins to be seen anywhere. How odd, thought Mother. This had never happened before.

She remembered Farmer Fred always had a good crop. Arriving at his farm, Mother noticed there were no pumpkins in the fields. The harvest must be over, she thought, and the pumpkins stored in his barn. That should make it easy to select a nice one.

She found Farmer Fred working on his tractor. "Good morning, Fred," said Mother Dog. "I would like to buy a nice pumpkin."

"I'm sorry, I have none," said Farmer Fred. "But Farmer Ned down the road might have some."

Farmer Ned did not have any pumpkins. Neither did Farmer Sally. Wherever Mother Dog went, there was not a pumpkin to be had. Oh my! Where had all the pumpkins gone? It would not be a perfect Thanksgiving if Father Dog did not get his pumpkin pie. She went to see Badger, who always had a wonderful orchard and vegetable patch.

"I'm sorry, Mother Dog. I have only a few turnips and acorn squash," said Badger.

"I'll take them," said Mother quickly, thankful for the few items.

Disappointed with her shopping trip, Mother Dog made her way home.

Postie had delivered the mail. There was an invitation from the Beavers that said, "Please join us for dinner on Thanksgiving Day at Beaver Pond."

How kind of the Beavers, thought Mother Dog, with a sigh of relief. The Beavers were sure to have pumpkin pie.

It could be a perfect Thanksgiving after all.

On Thanksgiving Day, Mother Dog was busy in the kitchen. She decided to take a tray of stuffed acorn squash and steamed turnips to the Beavers. Father Dog made some apple cider to take as a gift.

The Dog family was delighted to see so many good friends at Beaver Pond. It seemed all of Happytown had come to celebrate Thanksgiving Day with the Beavers.

Everyone had brought some food. The tables were full of fruit, berry bread, apple pies, acorns, seeds, nuts, and so much more. Mother Dog found a spot on the table for her tray. As she admired the variety of food, she noticed with dismay that there were no pumpkin pies.

It was not going to be a perfect Thanksgiving after all.

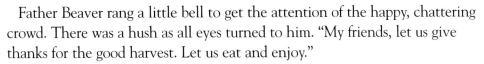

Father Beaver rang a little bell to get the attention of the happy, chattering crowd. There was a hush as all eyes turned to him. "My friends, let us give thanks for the good harvest. Let us eat and enjoy."

The residents of Happytown sat down to a magnificent feast. They ate and ate amid loud laughter and chatter. Mother Dog was delighted to see Father Dog having a wonderful time. Perhaps he would not miss his pumpkin pie.

The bell rang again. Officer Barney wanted everyone's attention. He was standing beside something that was covered by a big white sheet.

"I know many of you could not find any pumpkins for sale," he said. "I bought every one to make this surprise." He pulled back the white sheet to reveal the biggest pumpkin pie ever.

A gasp of admiration rose from the crowd!

A broad smile spread over Father Dog's face as he gazed at the enormous pie with anticipation.

Mother Dog gave a huge sigh of relief.

It was a perfect Thanksgiving Day after all.

DECEMBER: A Happy Sound

The Bears set out to get a Christmas tree. *Crunch* went their boots as they walked in the crisp snow. *Ching-aling* went the bells Mother Bear had attached to the sled. *Swish* went the polished runners as the sled glided along.

Children were playing hockey on a frozen pond. Their shouts and laughter had a happy sound. *Click, click, swoosh* went the skates as they glided around the glistening ice.

The tree farm was busy. Bonnie closed her eyes and listened to the sounds, the chip-chop of axes, the crunch of feet in the crisp snow, the happy sound of friends greeting friends.

The Bear family found the perfect tree. Father cut the tree and paid for it. Then they went to town to buy decorations.

The streets were busy with shoppers. Festive music wafted from shops as doors were opened. Santa's helper rang his bell. *Ching-aling!* "Merry Christmas!" he called.

"What are you doing?" Bertie asked when he saw Bonnie standing with her eyes closed.

"Listening to the happy sounds," she said.

Bertie closed his eyes. He smiled and nodded his head as he listened to the bells in the old steeple ringing a favorite carol.

"My goodness! The children look so tired," whispered Mother Bear to Father Bear.

Bertie didn't understand why Mother kindly declined his offer to pull the sled. Bonnie enjoyed a piggy-back all the way home.

At last it was Christmas Eve, and sounds of Christmas filled the Bear home. Logs crackled

and hissed as a fire burned brightly in the stone hearth. There was a happy bustle as wrapping paper rustled and scissors snipped while Father helped the children wrap presents.

"I'm wrapping my present to you! Don't peek, Bertie," said Bonnie as she grinned at her big brother.

"I'll close my eyes and listen to the sound," said Bertie with a big smile. After a moment, he added, "Listen! I can hear a noise outside."

The Bear children rushed to the window. They heard bells and the clip-clop of horse's hooves in the snow as a sleigh approached. A group of carolers dismounted from the sleigh. Gathering in front of the Bear house, they began to sing. Bonnie and Bertie closed their eyes as they listened to the beautiful sound of the carolers' voices.

"Children, why are your eyes closed? Do you feel all right?" asked Mother Bear, fussing about, checking their brows for fever.

"We're listening to the happy sounds of Christmas," said Bonnie.

Mother and Father Bear laughed, pleased that there was nothing wrong with their little ones. Then they closed their eyes. "Yes! Christmas does have the happiest sound," said Mother.

"Can we join the singing?" asked Bertie.

The Bears put on their winter jackets and went outside to sing with the carolers. And what a happy sound that was!